BigPig

Saves Valentine's Day

By Cecile Schoberle

 HarperFestival®
A Division of HarperCollins*Publishers*

He's the smallest in the family,
but he causes the most trouble.

I call my little brother BigPig.

BigPig, I'm trying to read!   No, no, no! Don't chew on my book!

I know all kinds of stuff.
I know that Valentine's Day is tomorrow.
And I know how to make cards for
my friends.

Bring back that ribbon!
Take those stickers off your
head! You silly willy, BigPig.

BigPig, don't touch anything!

Ooh, gross, BigPig!
Don't eat those dog biscuits.
That's not being good at all.

I get to go to school.
We're having a Valentine's Day party.
My little brother has to stay home.
He's too young to go.

Mommy shows me how to bake
sweetheart cookies.
I'll let you have one, BigPig,
but you must be good.

Be good while I'm gone, BigPig.
Don't touch any of my stuff!

Happy Valentine's Day, everybody!
Wait until you see what I made.

Be careful! That juice will spoil
my box of cards!

I have something wonderful
inside this box. Look.

The box is ruined! But where are the
cards? I know I put them in here!
Did I lose them on the way to school?
Are they still at home?

This is the saddest Valentine's Day I've ever had.
I have no cards to give my friends.

BigPig! You found my cards!
They're not lost!

Happy Valentine's Day, everyone.
Didn't I bake *yummy* cookies?

Oh, you're funny, BigPig.

Didn't I make beautiful cards?

"Isn't that sweet?"
says Mommy.

"You're your brother's favorite valentine."

Well, maybe *my* little brother's not *always* yucky—just most of the time.
Happy Valentine's Day, you sweet little ucky yucky BigPig!